A 4D BOOK

ADVENTURES IN MAKERSPACE

A BUILDING MISSION

WRITTEN BY
SHANNON MCCLINTOCK MILLER
AND
BLAKE HOENA

ILLUSTRATED BY
ALAN BROWN

STONE ARCH BOOKS
a capstone imprint

capstone®

www.mycapstone.com

A Building Mission is published by Stone Arch Books,
a Capstone imprint
1710 Roe Crest Drive, North Mankato, Minnesota 56003
www.mycapstonepub.com

Library of Congress Cataloging-in-Publication Data
Names: Miller, Shannon (Shannon McClintock), author. | Hoena, B. A., author. | Brown, Alan (Illustrator), illustrator.
Title: A building mission / by Shannon McClintock Miller and Blake Hoena ; illustrated by Alan Brown.
Description: North Mankato, Minnesota : Stone Arch Books, [2019] | Series: Adventures in makerspace | Audience: Ages 8-10.
Identifiers: LCCN 2018044111 | ISBN 9781496579485 (hardcover) | ISBN 9781496579522 (pbk.) | ISBN 9781496579560 (ebook pdf)
Subjects: LCSH: Tall buildings--Design and construction--Juvenile literature. | Architecture--Juvenile literature. | Space Needle (Seattle, Wash.)--Juvenile literature. | Makerspaces--Juvenile literature. | LCGFT: Graphic novels.
Classification: LCC TH1615 .M55 2019 | DDC 720/.483--dc23 LC record available at https://lccn.loc.gov/2018044111

Book design and art direction: Mighty Media
Editorial direction: Kellie M. Hultgren
Music direction: Elizabeth Draper
Music written and produced by Mark Mallman

Printed and bound in the United States of America
PA48

CONTENTS

1 Ask an adult to download the app.    Capstone 4D Education

2 Scan any page with the star.

3 Enjoy your cool stuff!

—— OR ——

Use this password at capstone4D.com

build.79485

MEET THE SPECIALIST

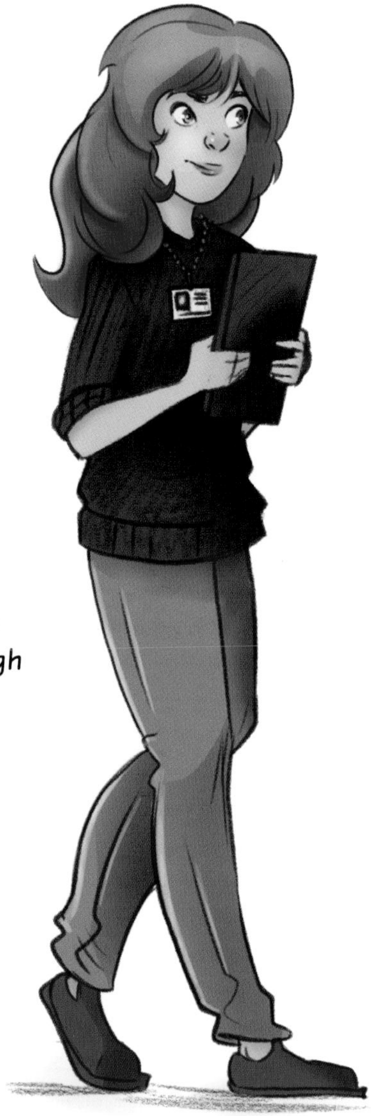

ABILITIES:
speed reader, tech titan, foreign language master, traveler through literature and history

MS. GILLIAN

TEACHER-LIBRARIAN

MEET THE STUDENTS

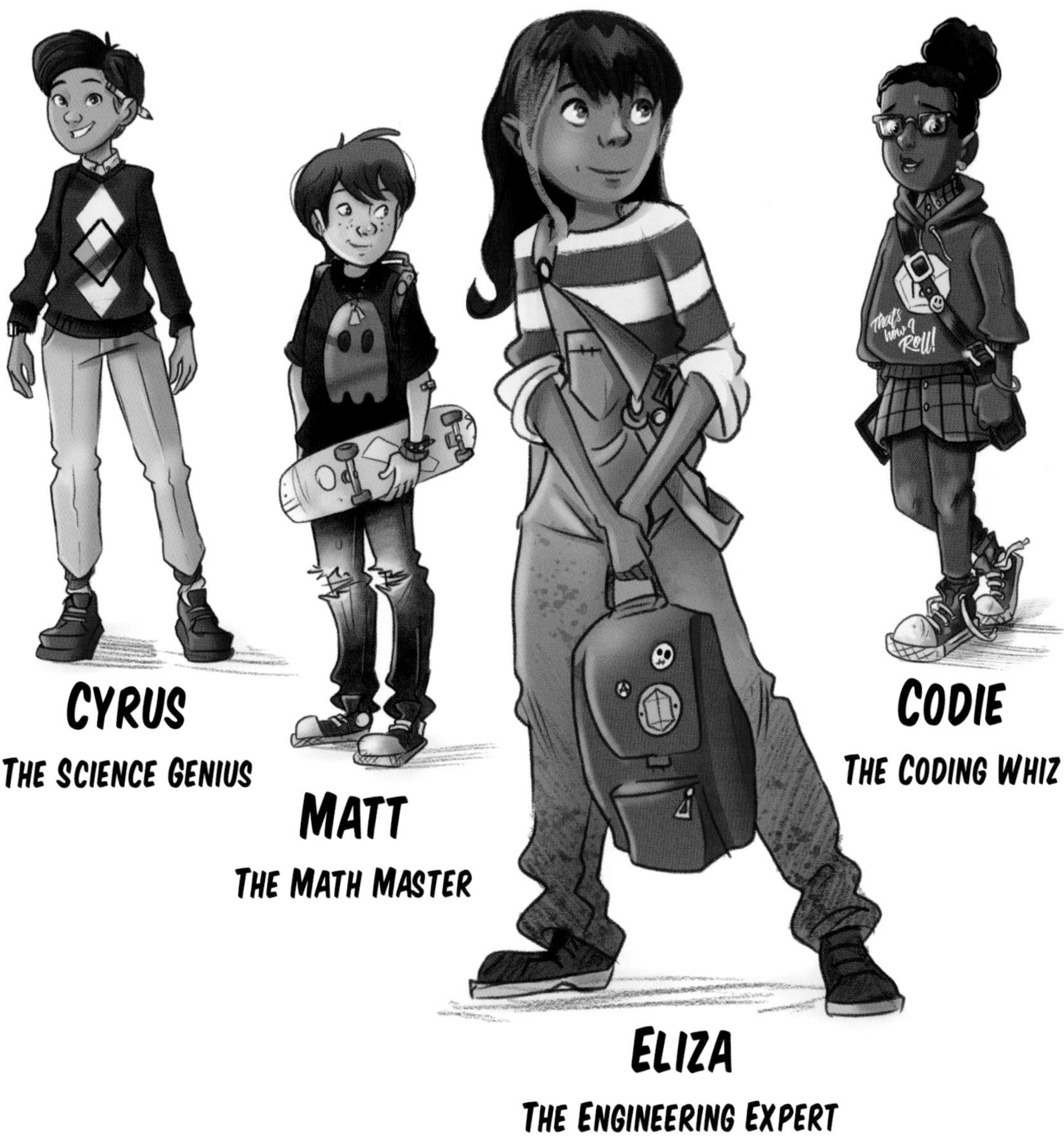
CYRUS
THE SCIENCE GENIUS
MATT
THE MATH MASTER
ELIZA
THE ENGINEERING EXPERT
CODIE
THE CODING WHIZ

NEWSPAPER CHALLENGE

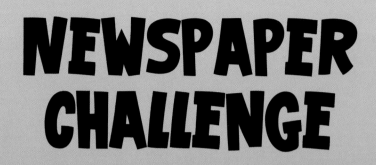

ELIZA AND HER FRIENDS ARE BRINGING STACKS OF NEWSPAPERS TO THEIR FAVORITE PLACE IN EMERSON ELEMENTARY. AT THE BACK OF THE SCHOOL'S LIBRARY IS AN AREA THAT MS. GILLIAN CALLS THE MAKERSPACE.

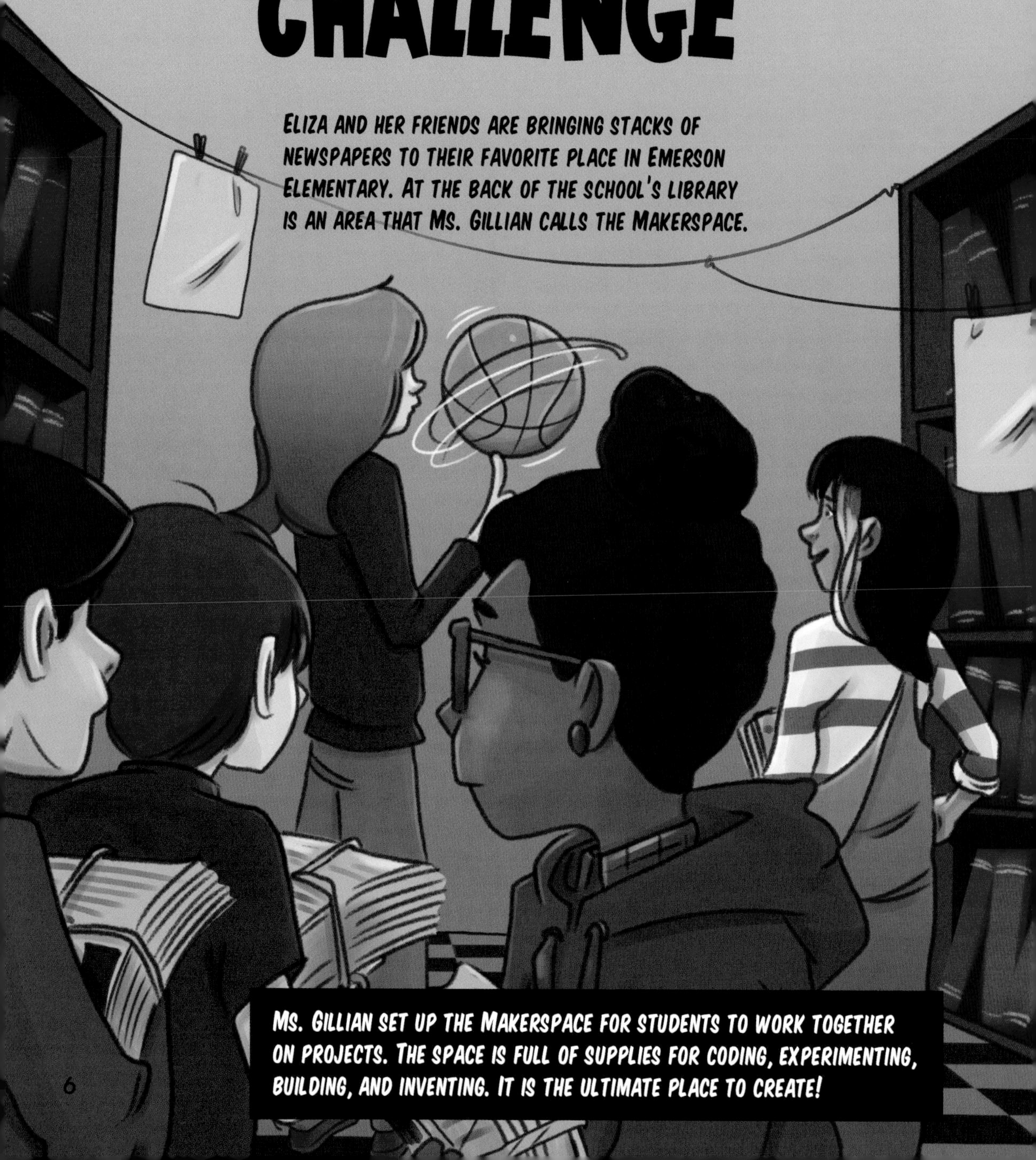

MS. GILLIAN SET UP THE MAKERSPACE FOR STUDENTS TO WORK TOGETHER ON PROJECTS. THE SPACE IS FULL OF SUPPLIES FOR CODING, EXPERIMENTING, BUILDING, AND INVENTING. IT IS THE ULTIMATE PLACE TO CREATE!

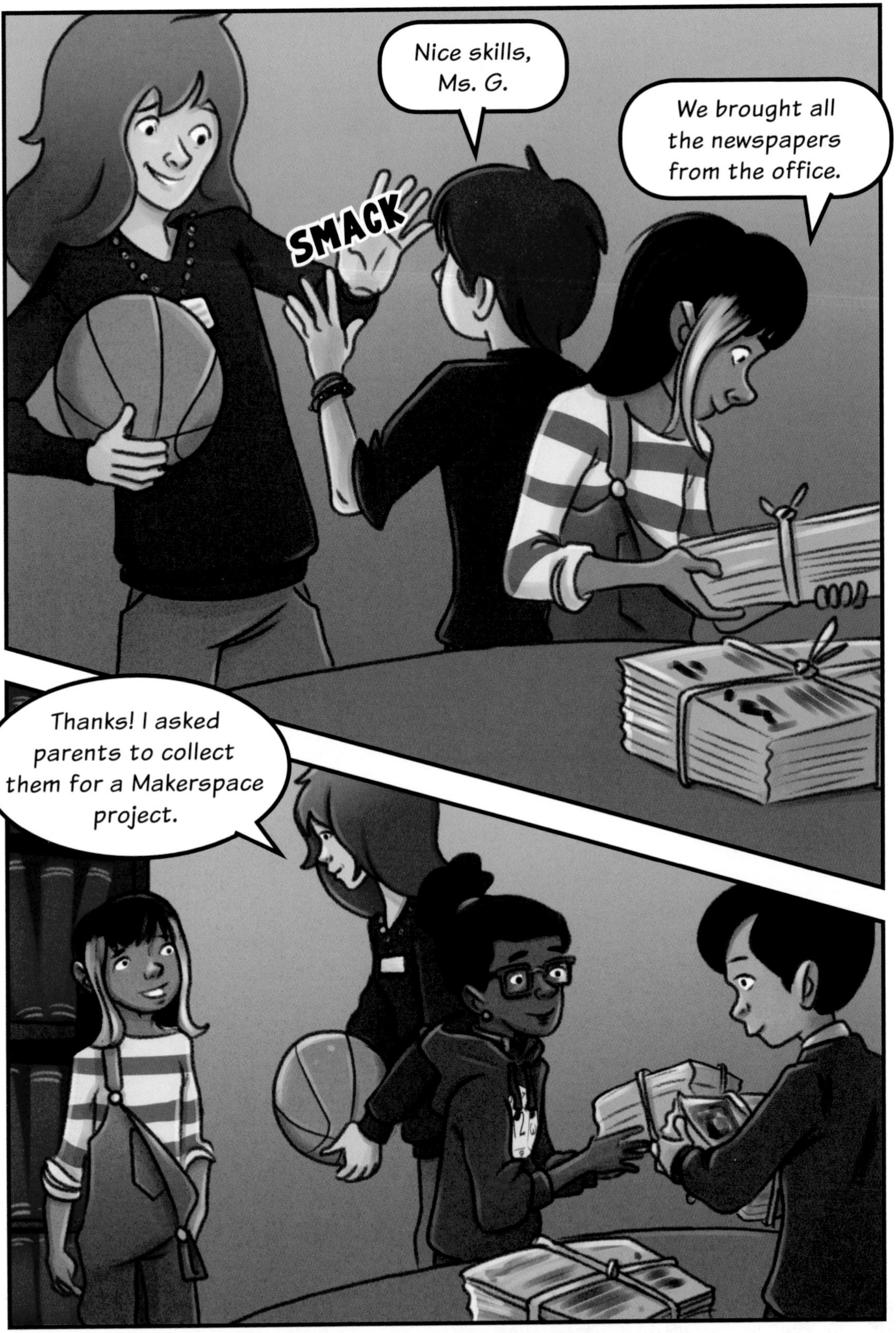
Nice skills, Ms. G.
SMACK
We brought all the newspapers from the office.
Thanks! I asked parents to collect them for a Makerspace project.

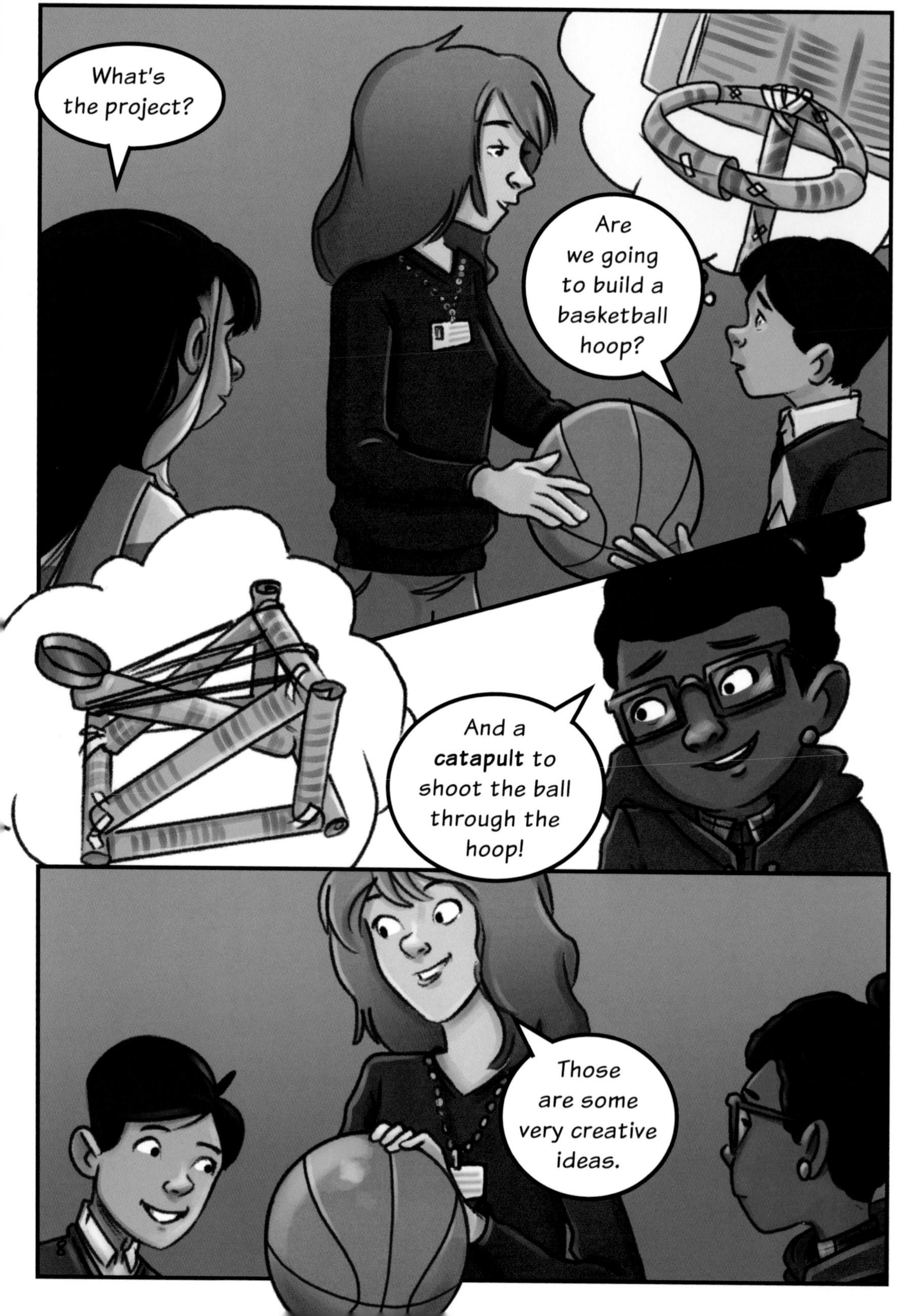
What's the project?
Are we going to build a basketball hoop?
And a **catapult** to shoot the ball through the hoop!
Those are some very creative ideas.

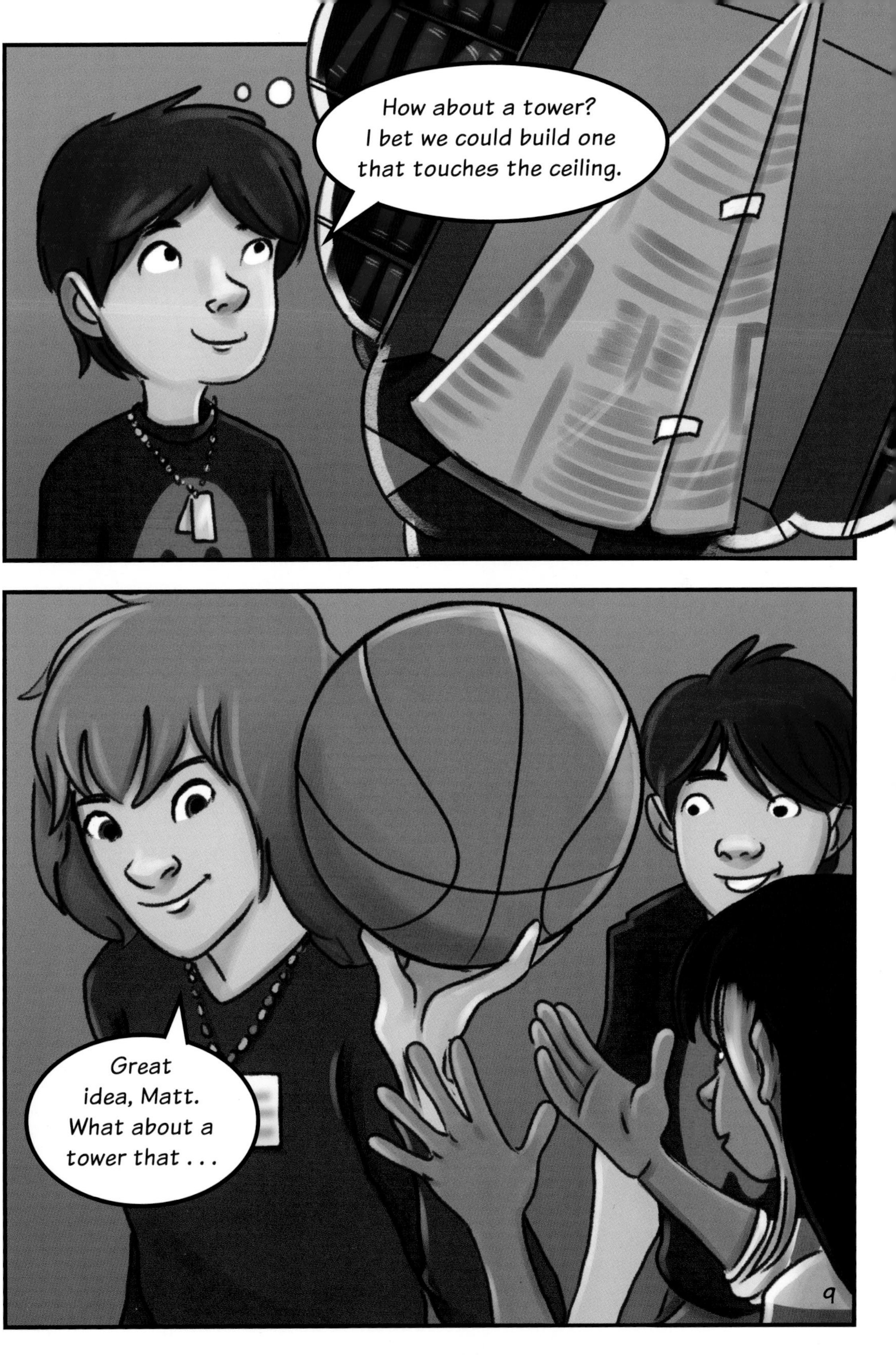
How about a tower? I bet we could build one that touches the ceiling.
Great idea, Matt. What about a tower that . . .

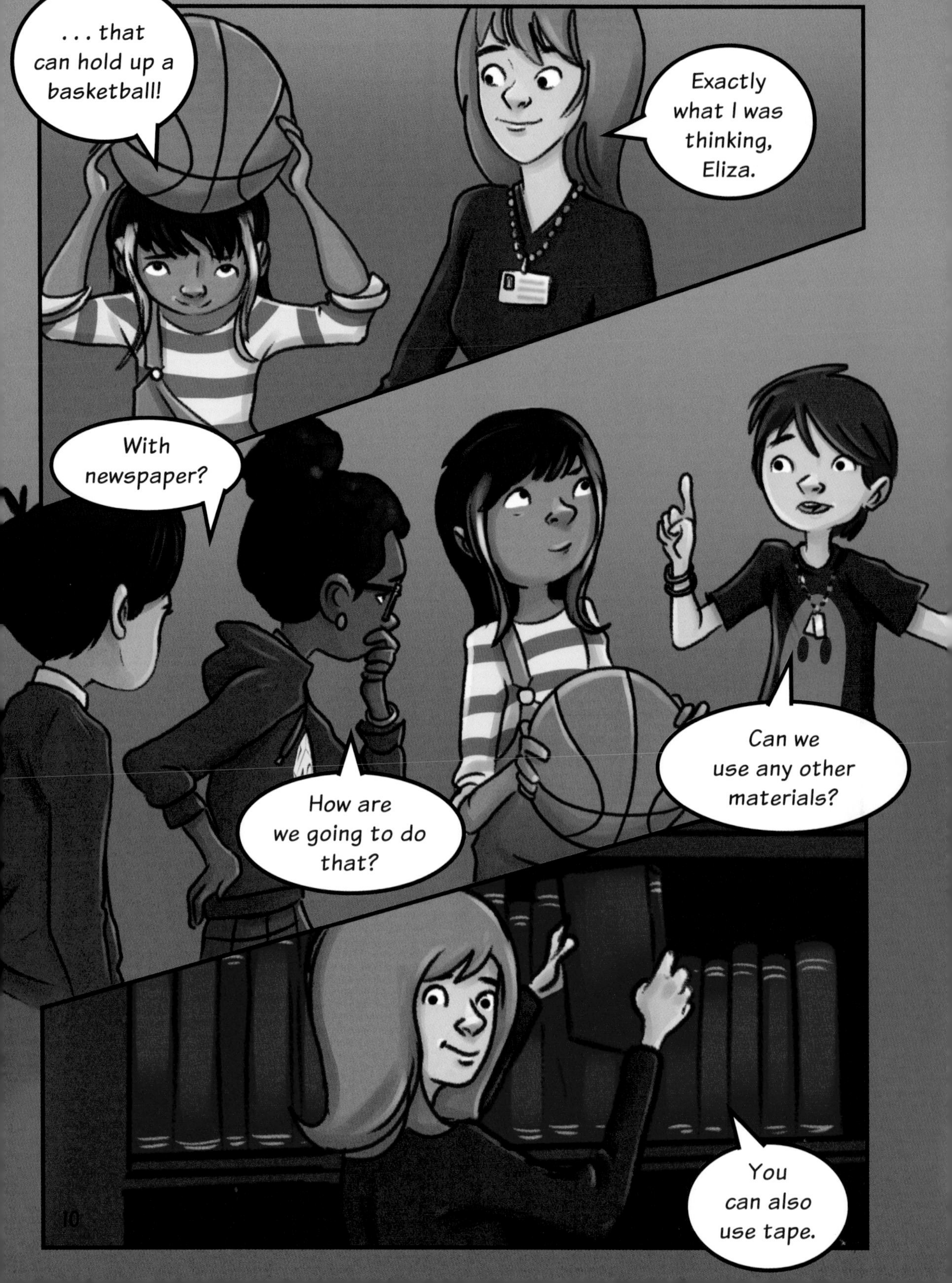
. . . that can hold up a basketball!
Exactly what I was thinking, Eliza.
With newspaper?
How are we going to do that?
Can we use any other materials?
You can also use tape.

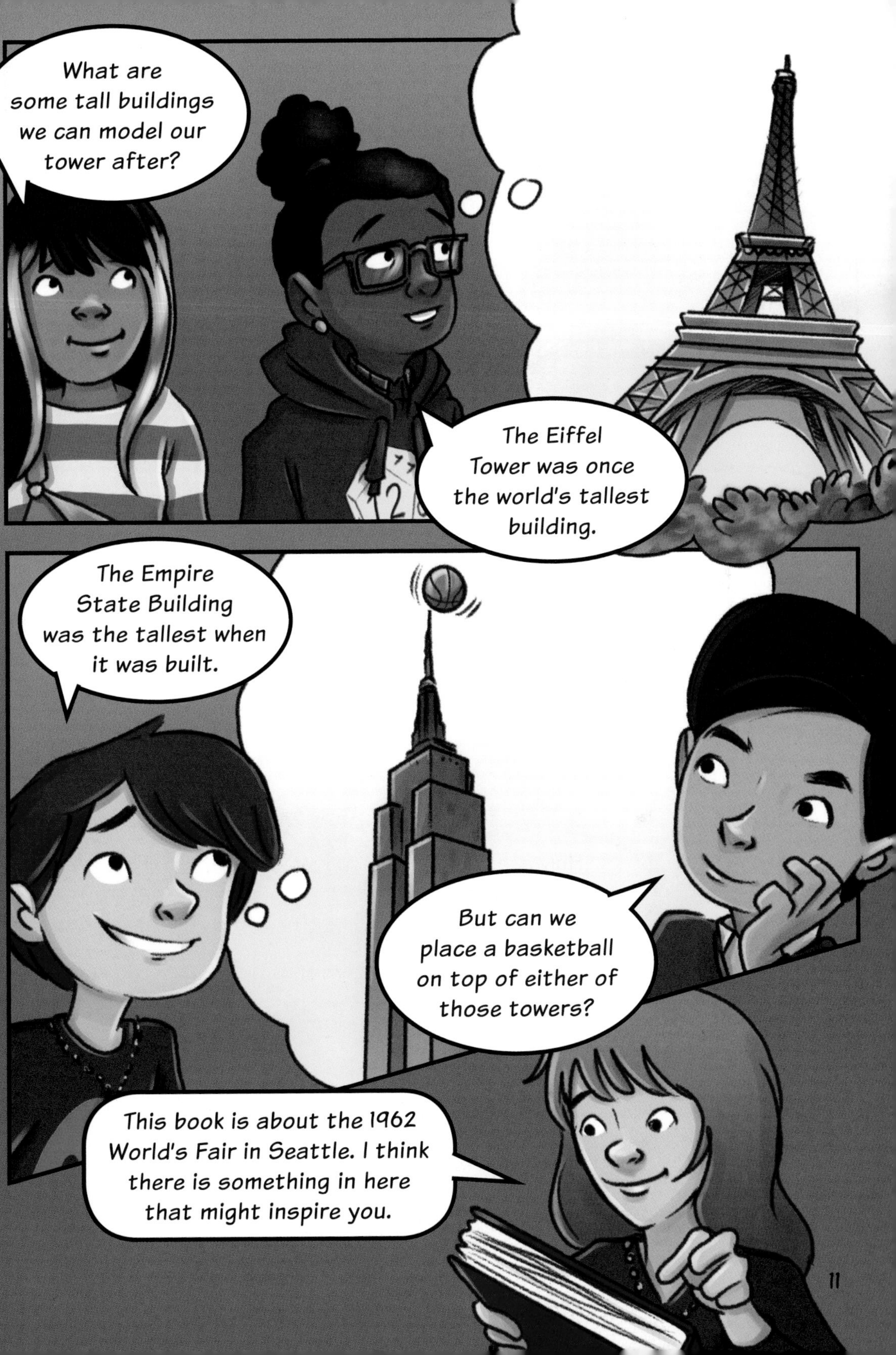
What are some tall buildings we can model our tower after?
The Eiffel Tower was once the world's tallest building.
The Empire State Building was the tallest when it was built.
But can we place a basketball on top of either of those towers?
This book is about the 1962 World's Fair in Seattle. I think there is something in here that might inspire you.

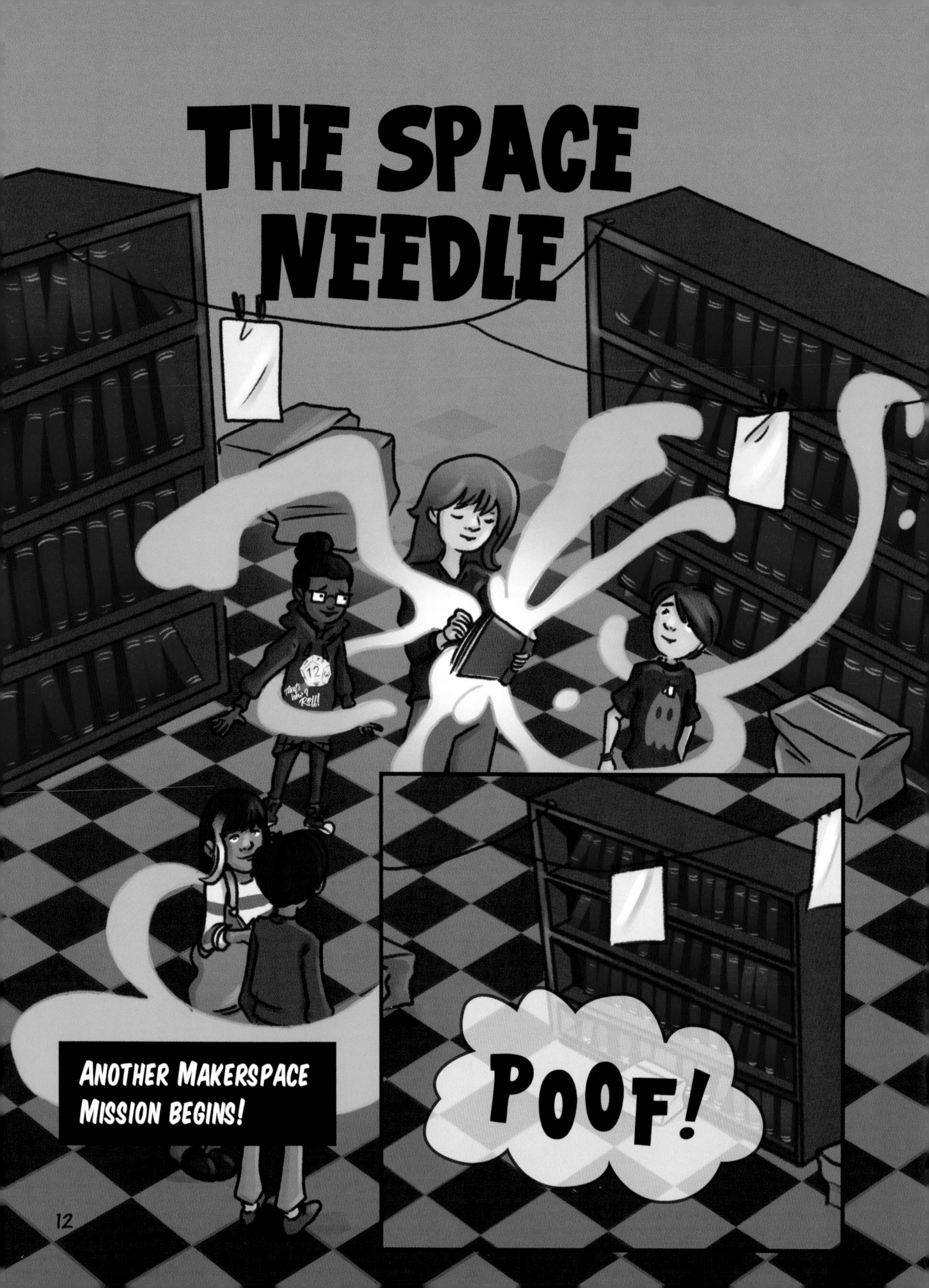
THE SPACE NEEDLE
ANOTHER MAKERSPACE MISSION BEGINS!
POOF!

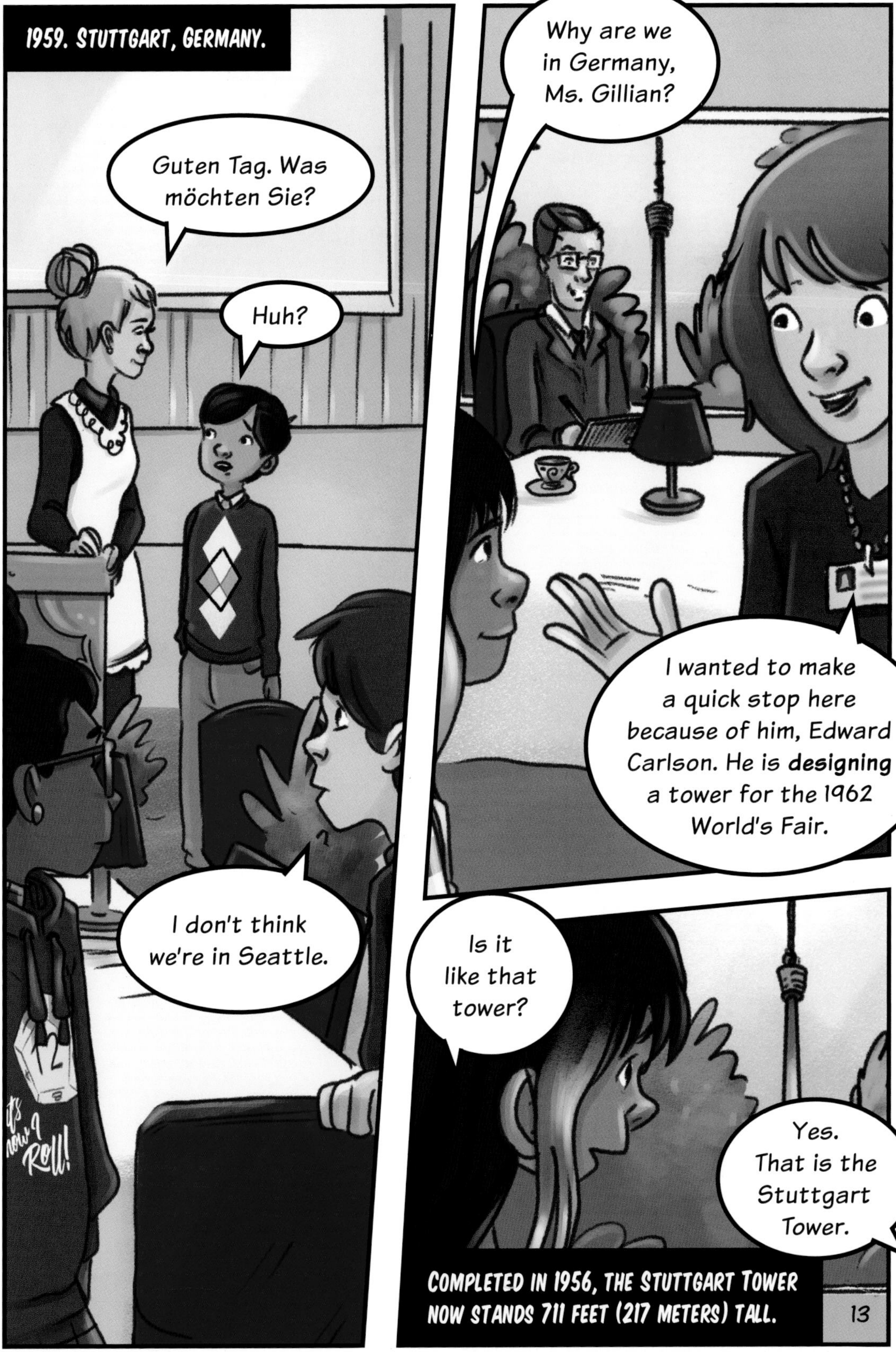
1959. STUTTGART, GERMANY.
Guten Tag. Was möchten Sie?
Huh?
I don't think we're in Seattle.
Why are we in Germany, Ms. Gillian?
I wanted to make a quick stop here because of him, Edward Carlson. He is designing a tower for the 1962 World's Fair.
Is it like that tower?
Yes. That is the Stuttgart Tower.
COMPLETED IN 1956, THE STUTTGART TOWER NOW STANDS 711 FEET (217 METERS) TALL.

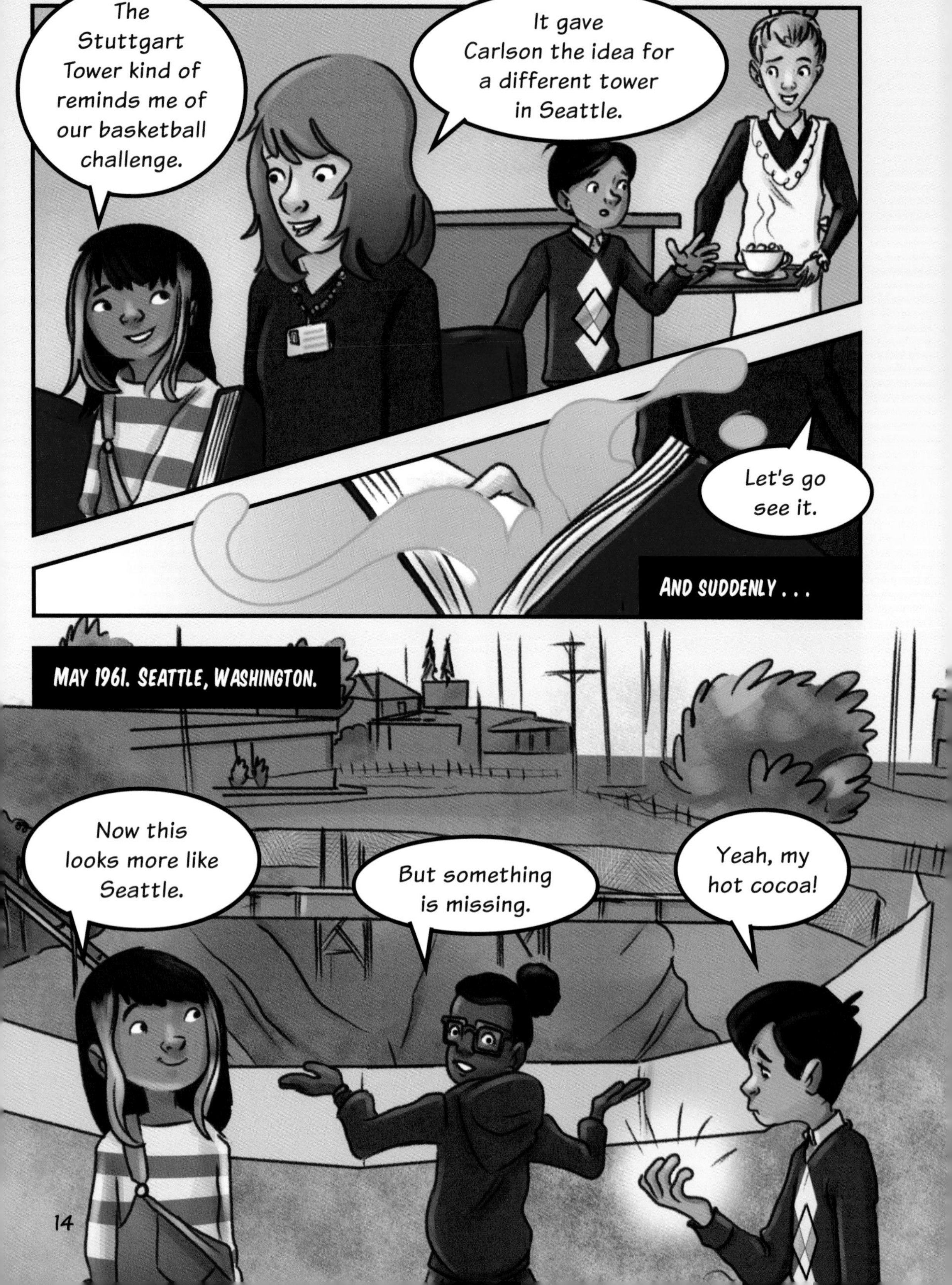
The Stuttgart Tower kind of reminds me of our basketball challenge.
It gave Carlson the idea for a different tower in Seattle.
Let's go see it.
AND SUDDENLY . . .
MAY 1961. SEATTLE, WASHINGTON.
Now this looks more like Seattle.
But something is missing.
Yeah, my hot cocoa!

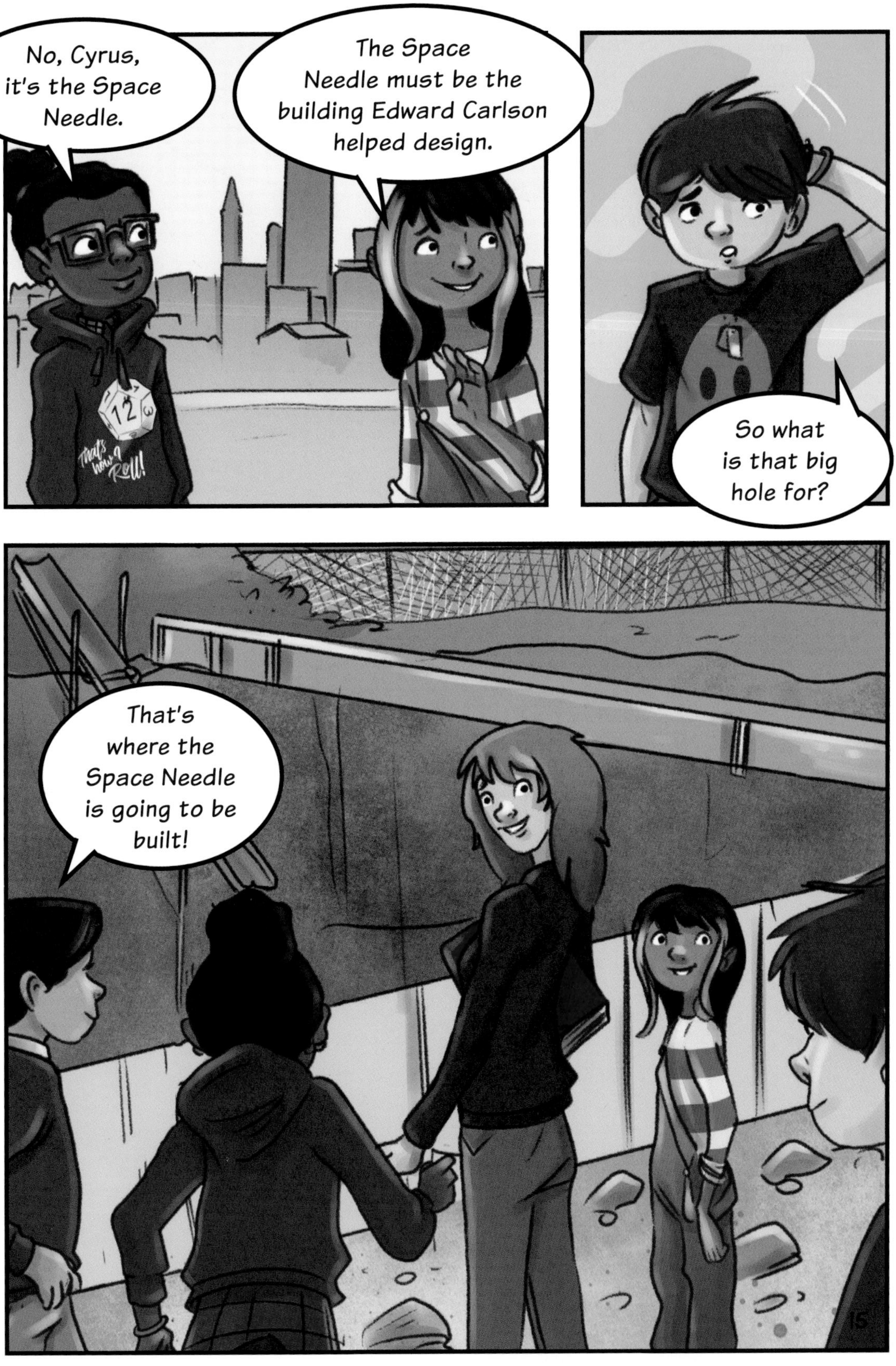
No, Cyrus, it's the Space Needle.
The Space Needle must be the building Edward Carlson helped design.
So what is that big hole for?
That's where the Space Needle is going to be built!

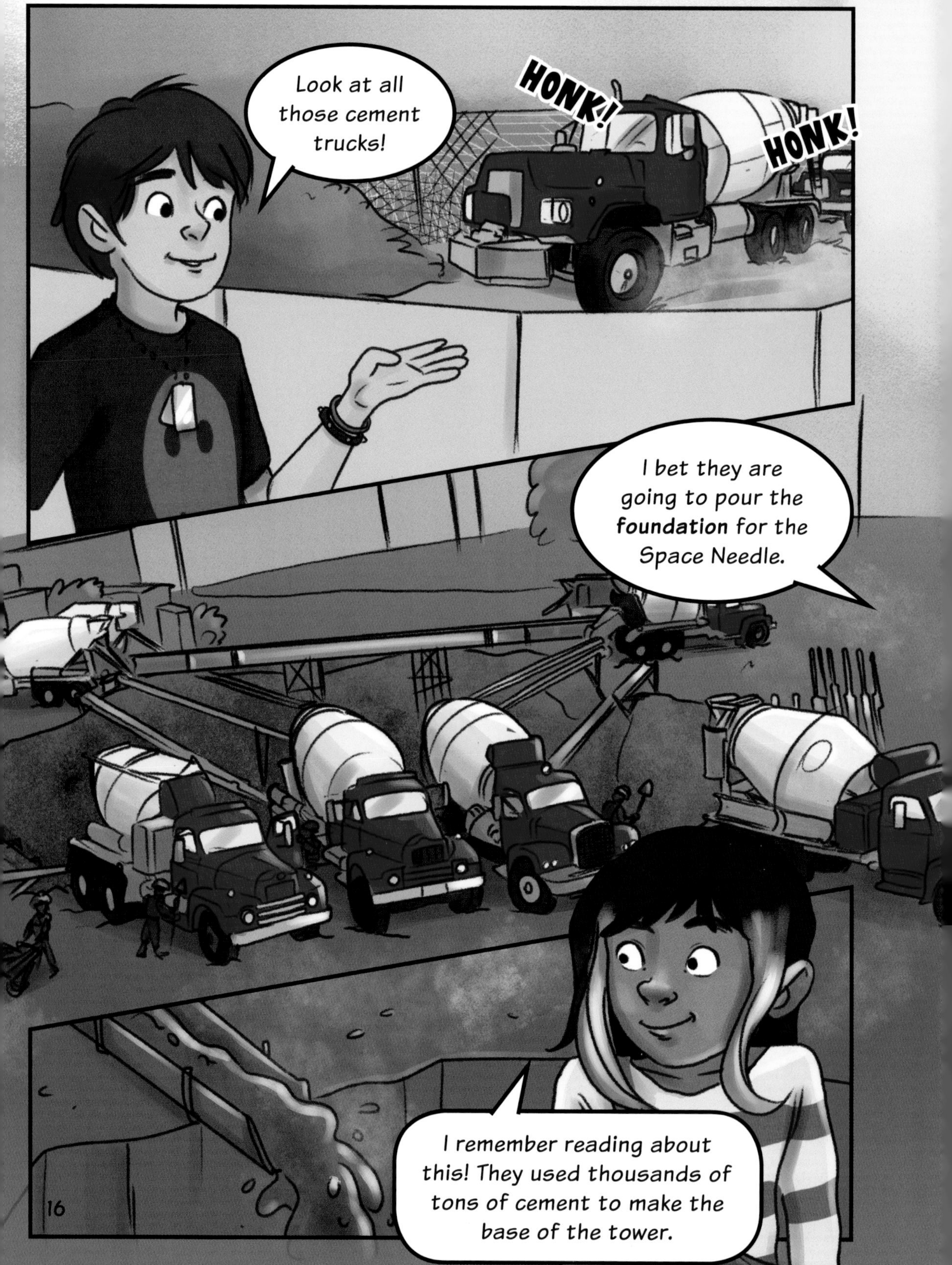
Look at all those cement trucks!
HONK!
HONK!
I bet they are going to pour the **foundation** for the Space Needle.
I remember reading about this! They used thousands of tons of cement to make the base of the tower.

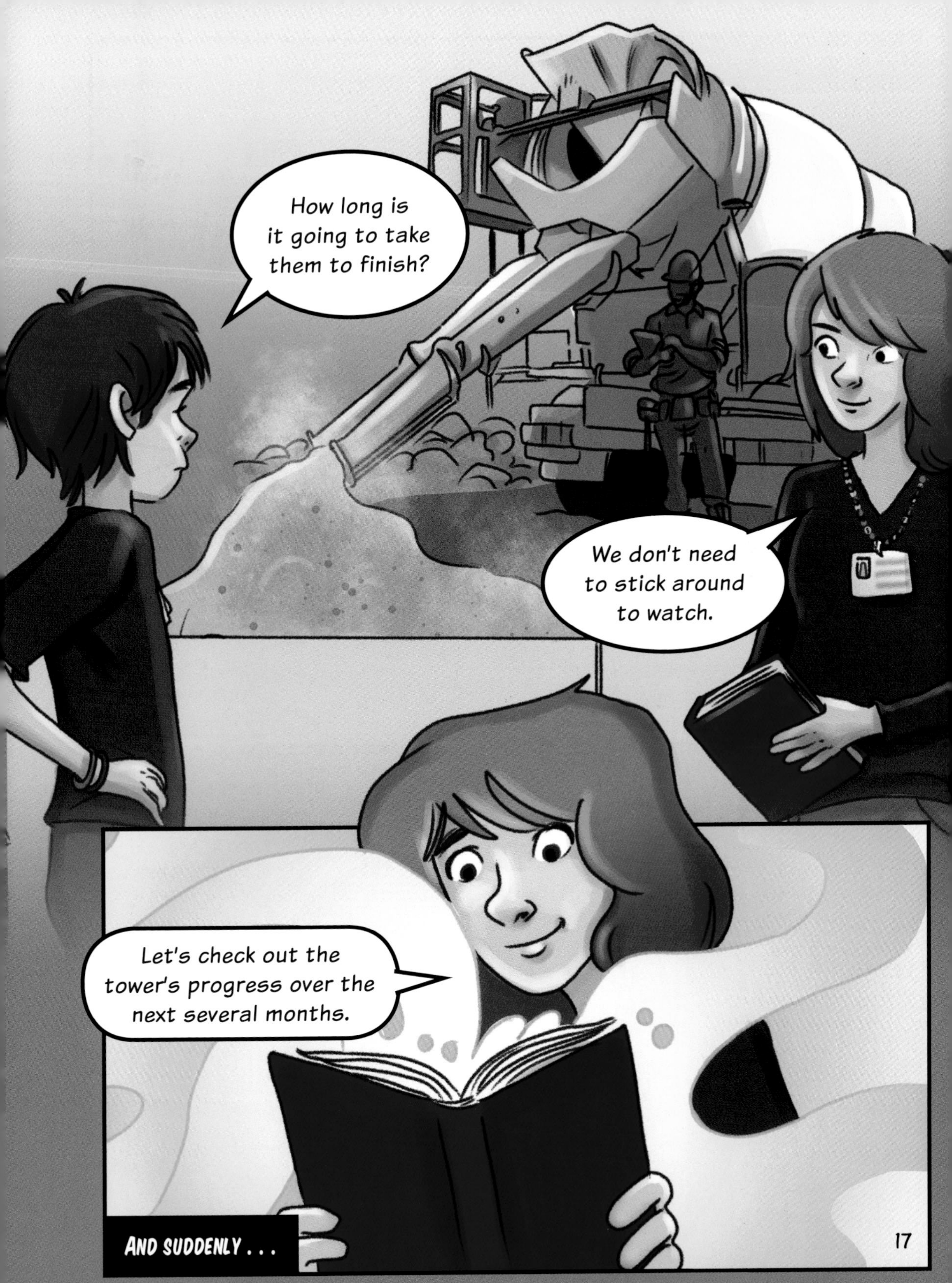
How long is it going to take them to finish?
We don't need to stick around to watch.
Let's check out the tower's progress over the next several months.
AND SUDDENLY . . .

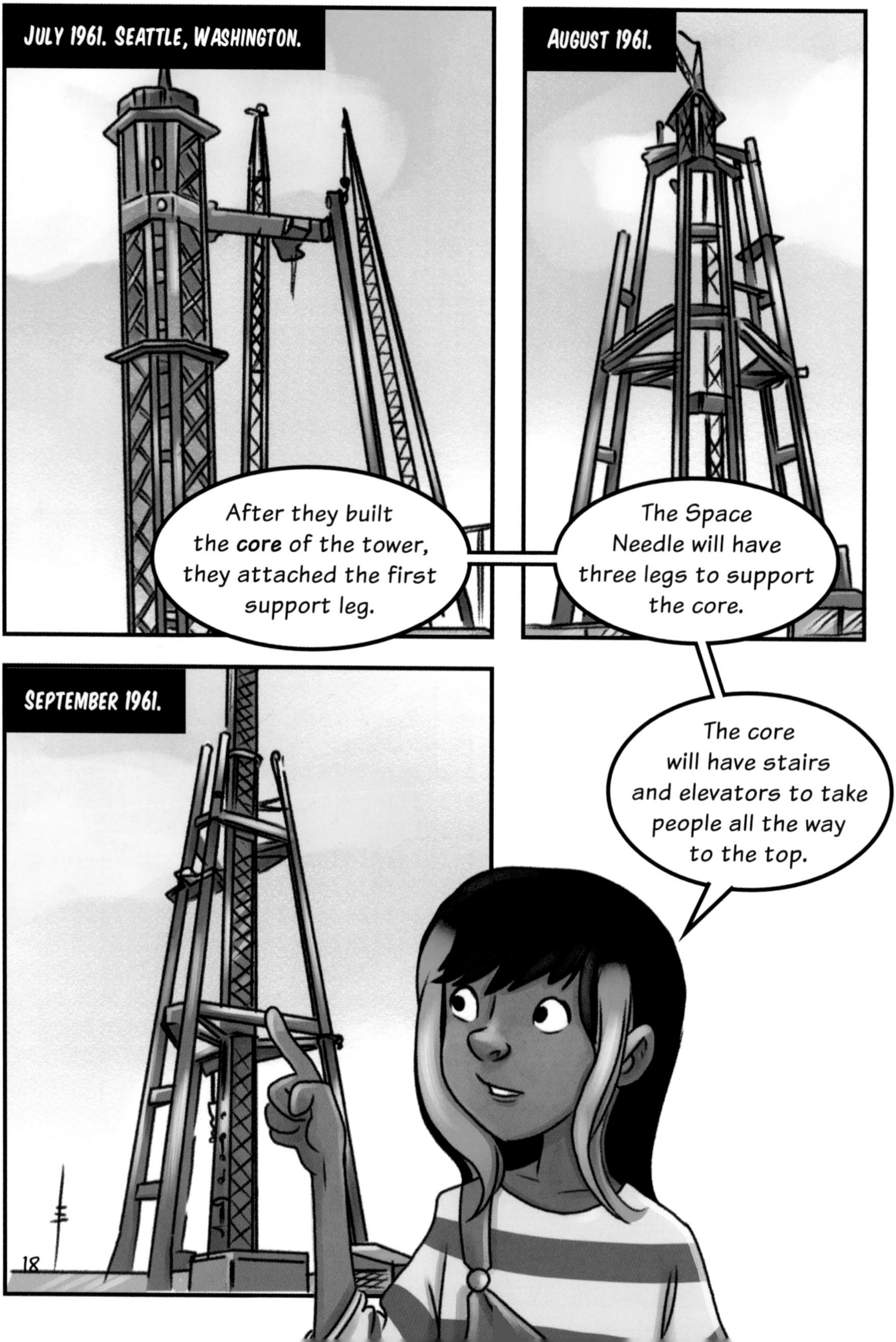
JULY 1961. SEATTLE, WASHINGTON.
AUGUST 1961.
After they built the **core** of the tower, they attached the first support leg.
The Space Needle will have three legs to support the core.
SEPTEMBER 1961.
The core will have stairs and elevators to take people all the way to the top.

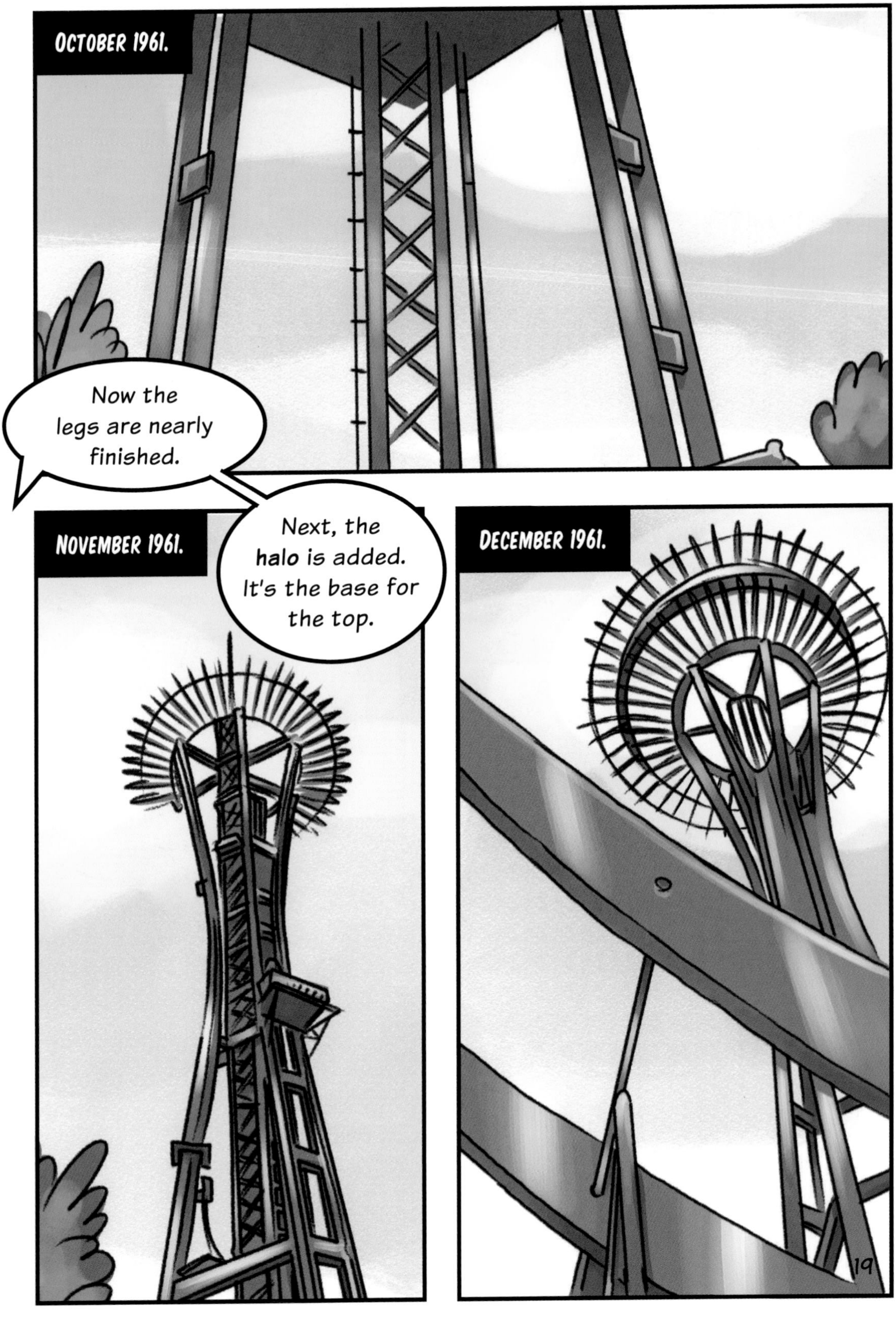
OCTOBER 1961.
Now the legs are nearly finished.
NOVEMBER 1961.
Next, the **halo** is added. It's the base for the top.
DECEMBER 1961.

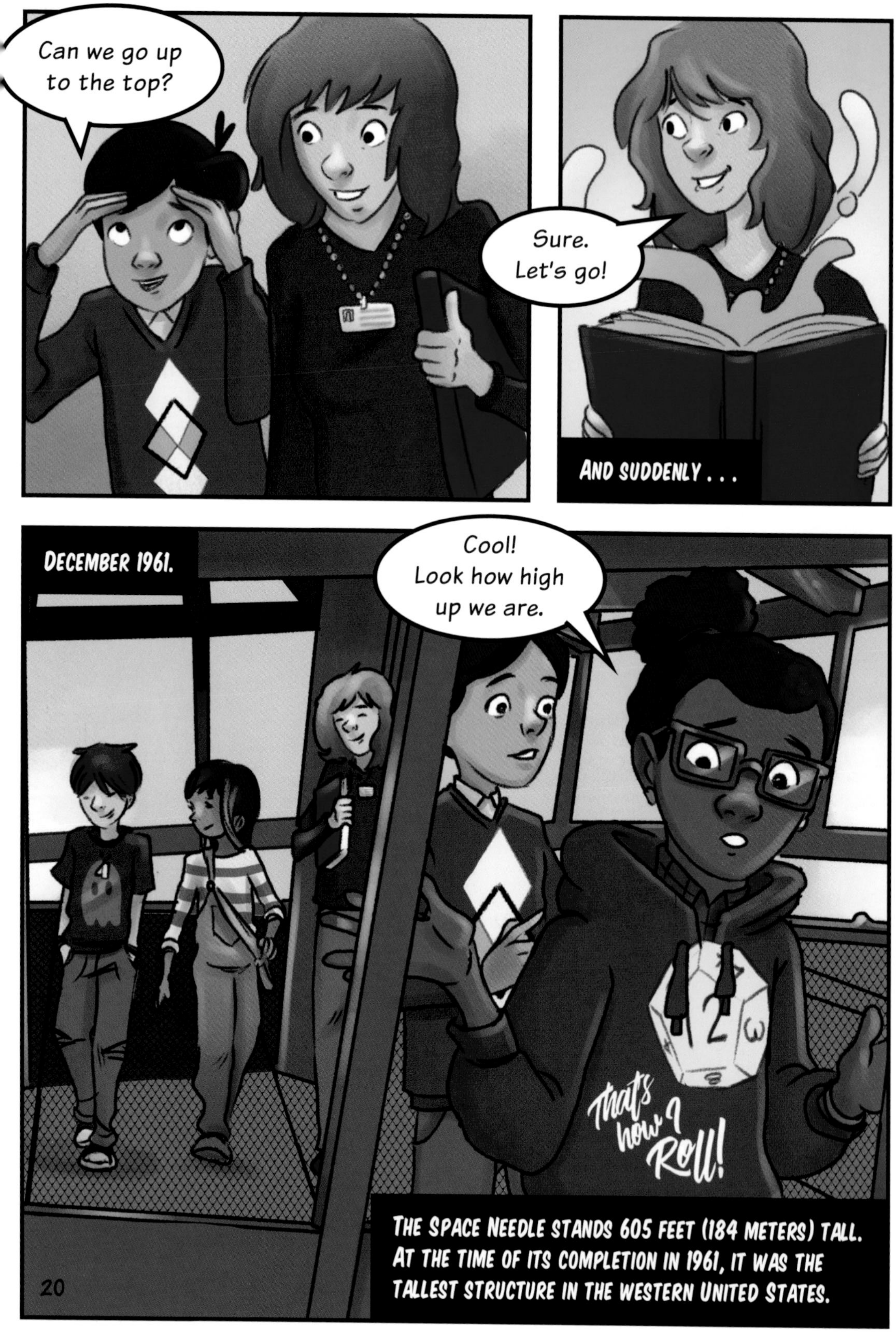
Can we go up to the top?
Sure. Let's go!
AND SUDDENLY . . .
DECEMBER 1961.
Cool! Look how high up we are.
That's how I Roll!
THE SPACE NEEDLE STANDS 605 FEET (184 METERS) TALL. AT THE TIME OF ITS COMPLETION IN 1961, IT WAS THE TALLEST STRUCTURE IN THE WESTERN UNITED STATES.

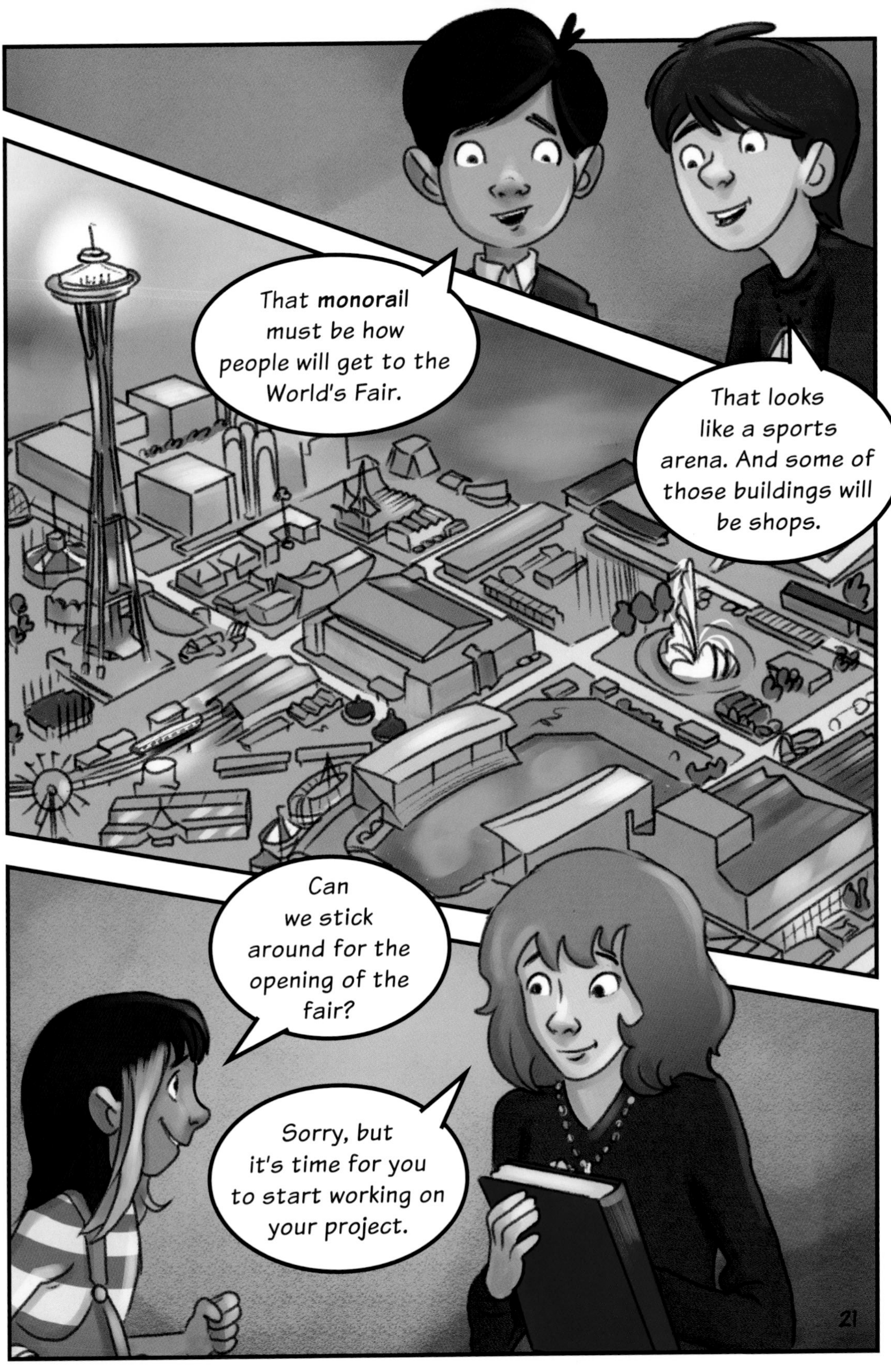
That **monorail** must be how people will get to the World's Fair.
That looks like a sports arena. And some of those buildings will be shops.
Can we stick around for the opening of the fair?
Sorry, but it's time for you to start working on your project.

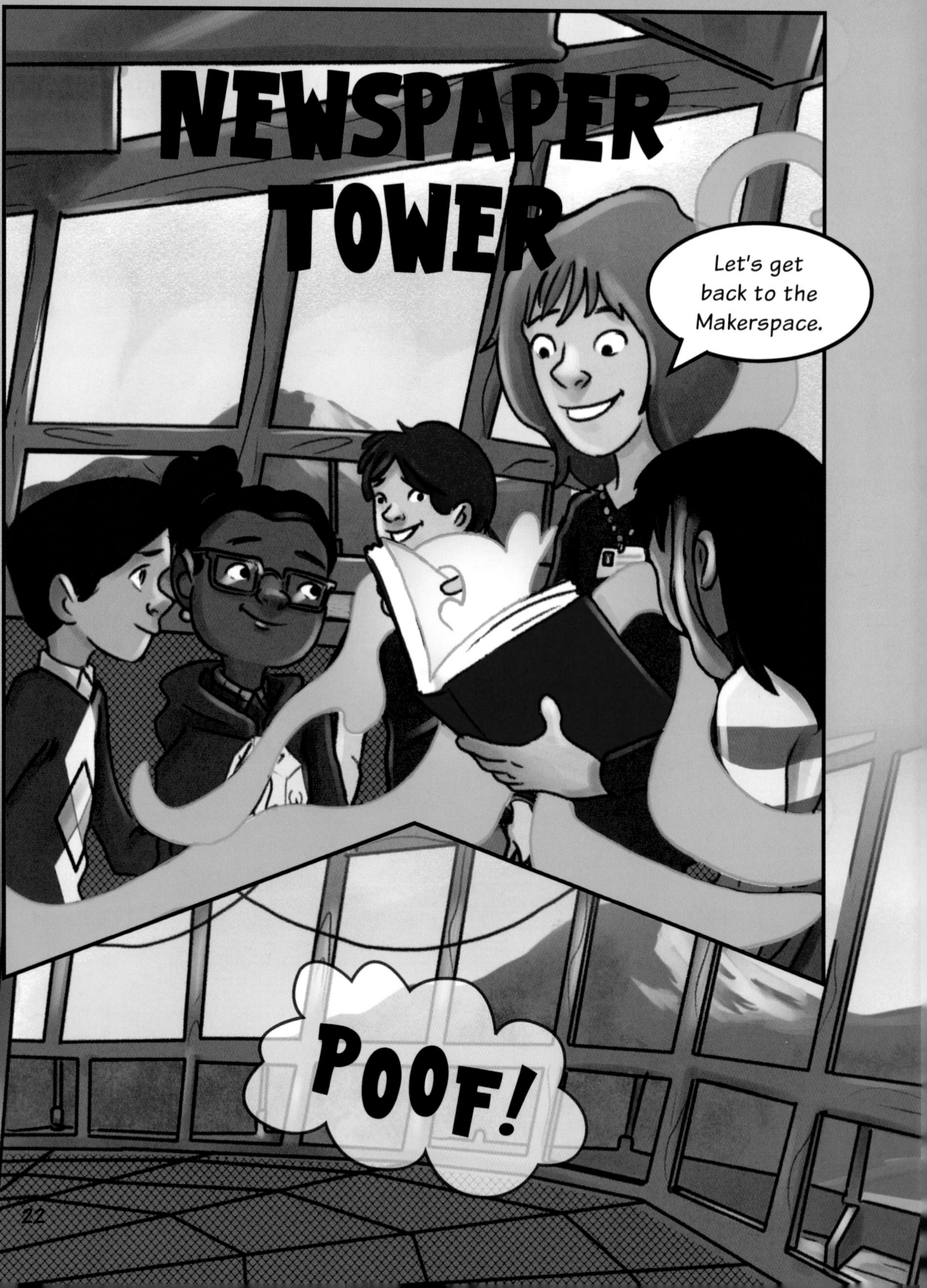
NEWSPAPER TOWER
Let's get back to the Makerspace.
POOF!

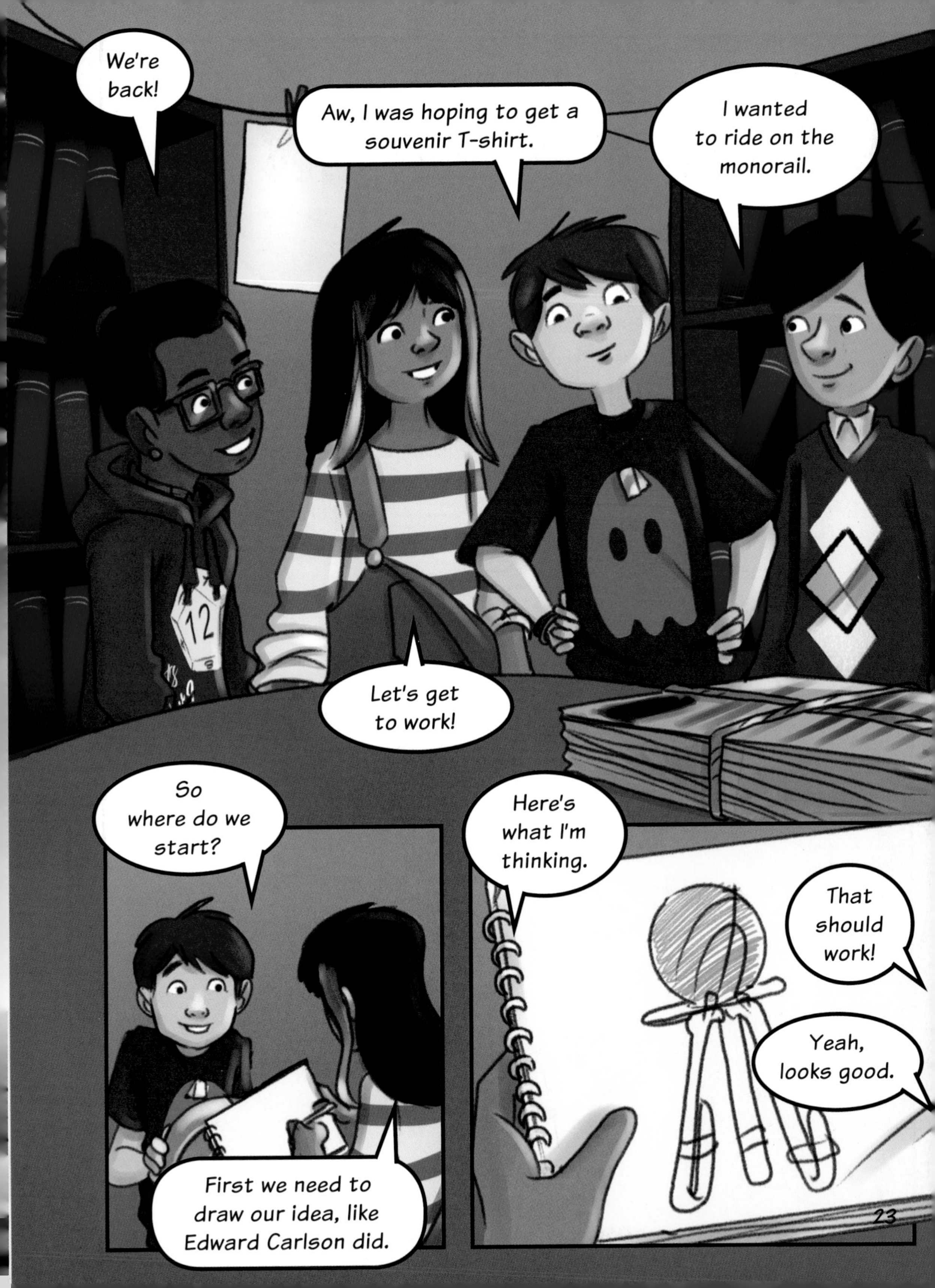
We're back!
Aw, I was hoping to get a souvenir T-shirt.
I wanted to ride on the monorail.
Let's get to work!
So where do we start?
First we need to draw our idea, like Edward Carlson did.
Here's what I'm thinking.
That should work!
Yeah, looks good.

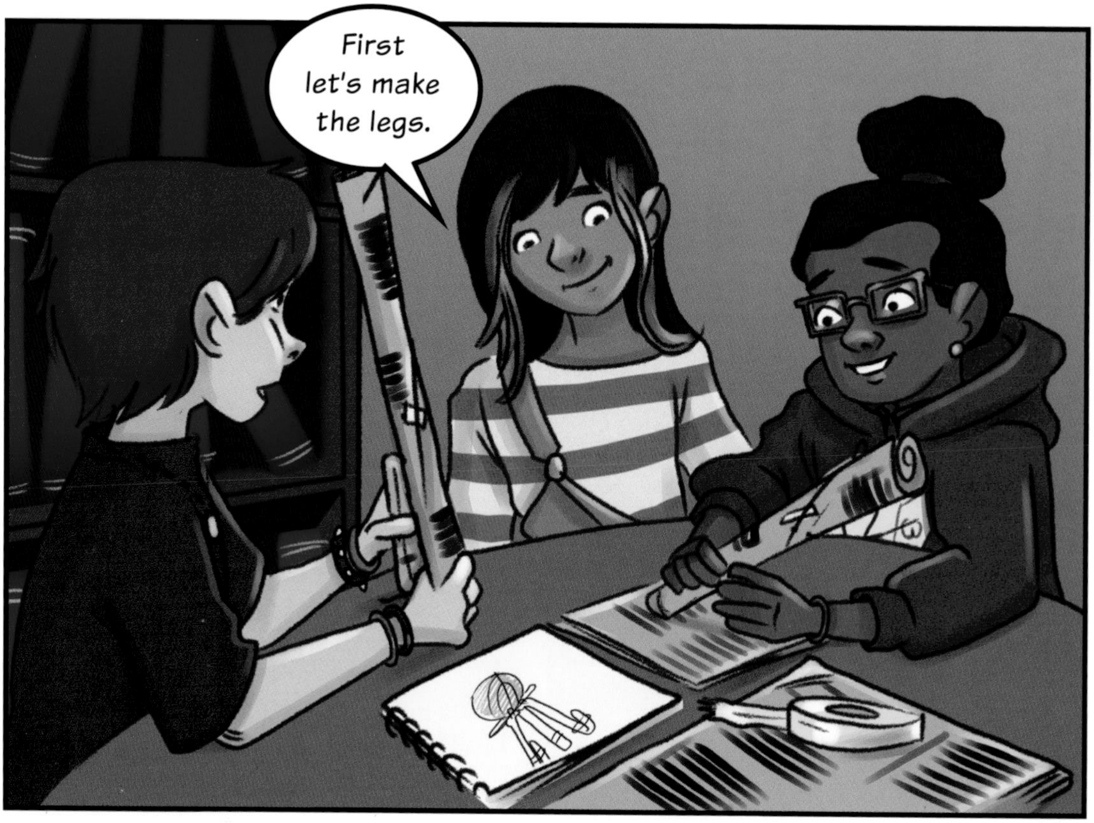
First let's make the legs.

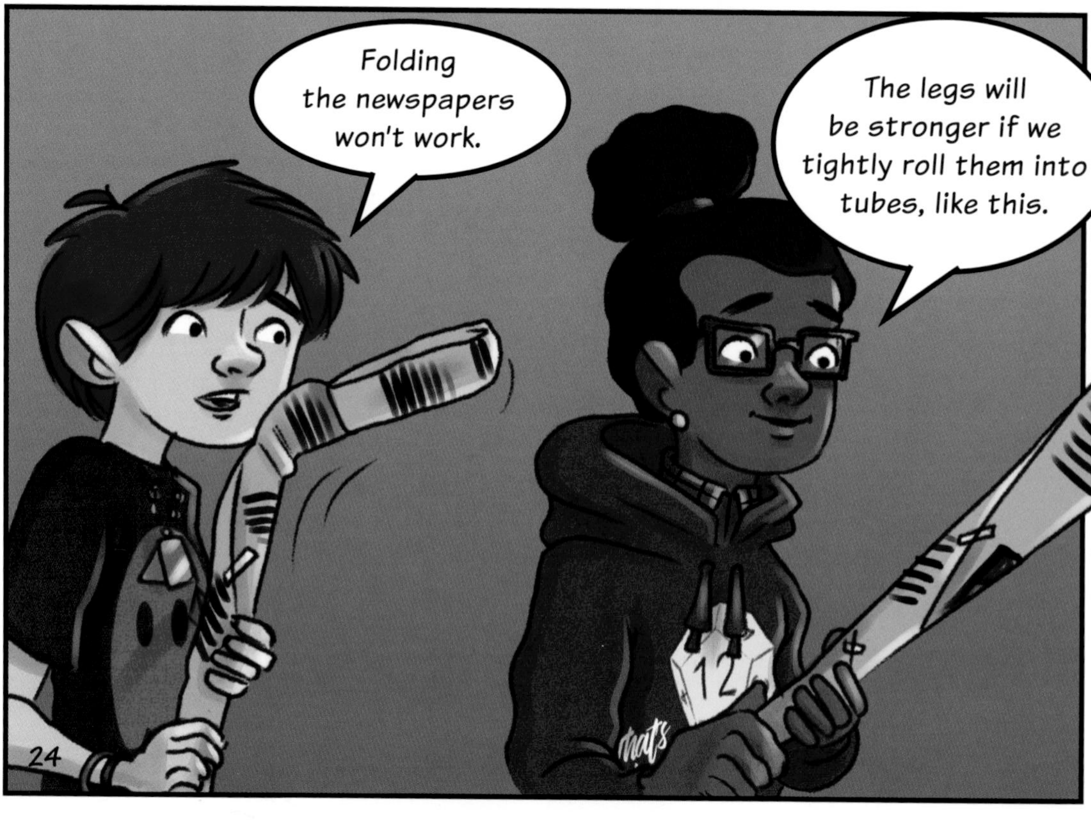
Folding the newspapers won't work.
The legs will be stronger if we tightly roll them into tubes, like this.

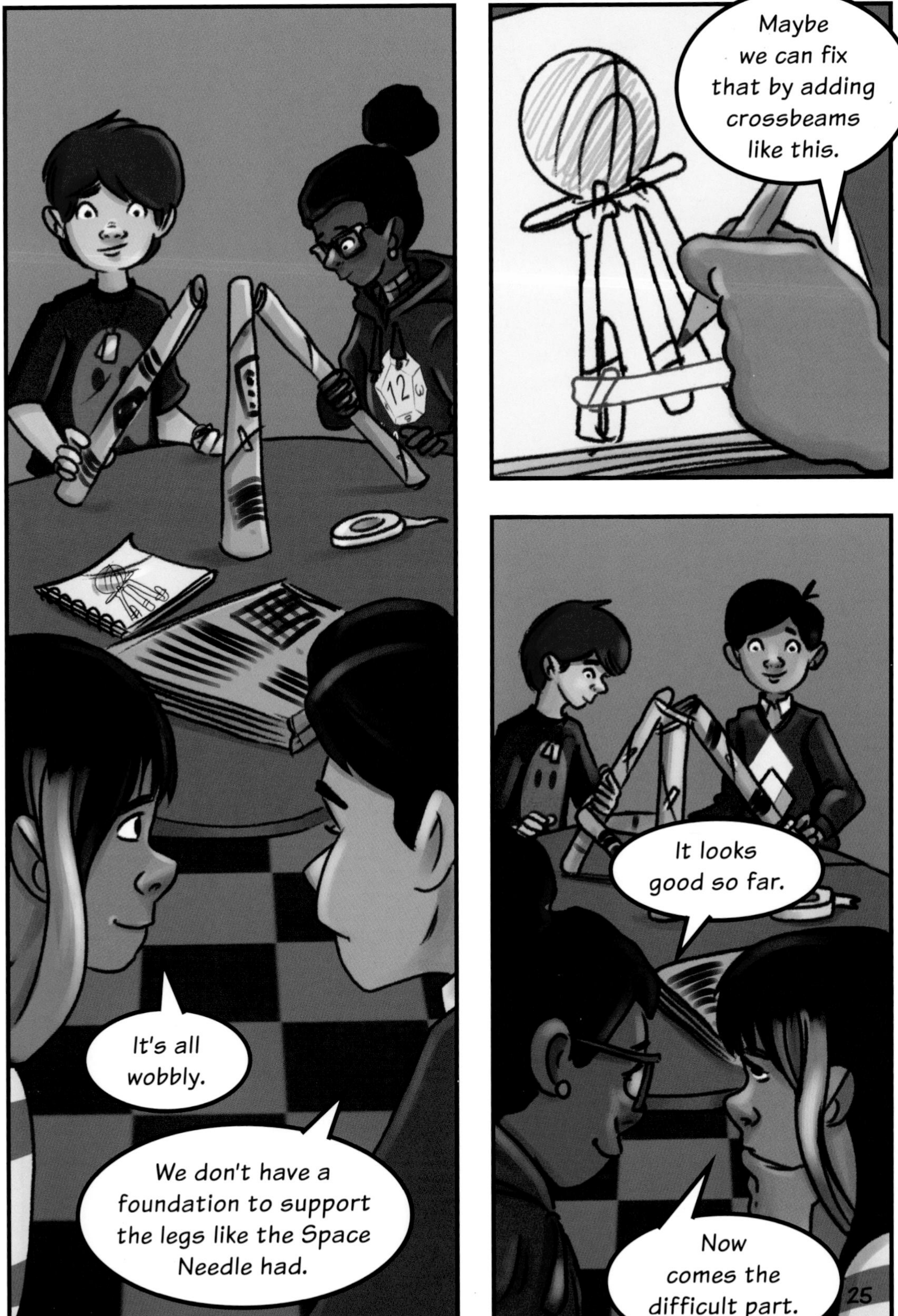
It's all wobbly.
We don't have a foundation to support the legs like the Space Needle had.
Maybe we can fix that by adding crossbeams like this.
It looks good so far.
Now comes the difficult part.

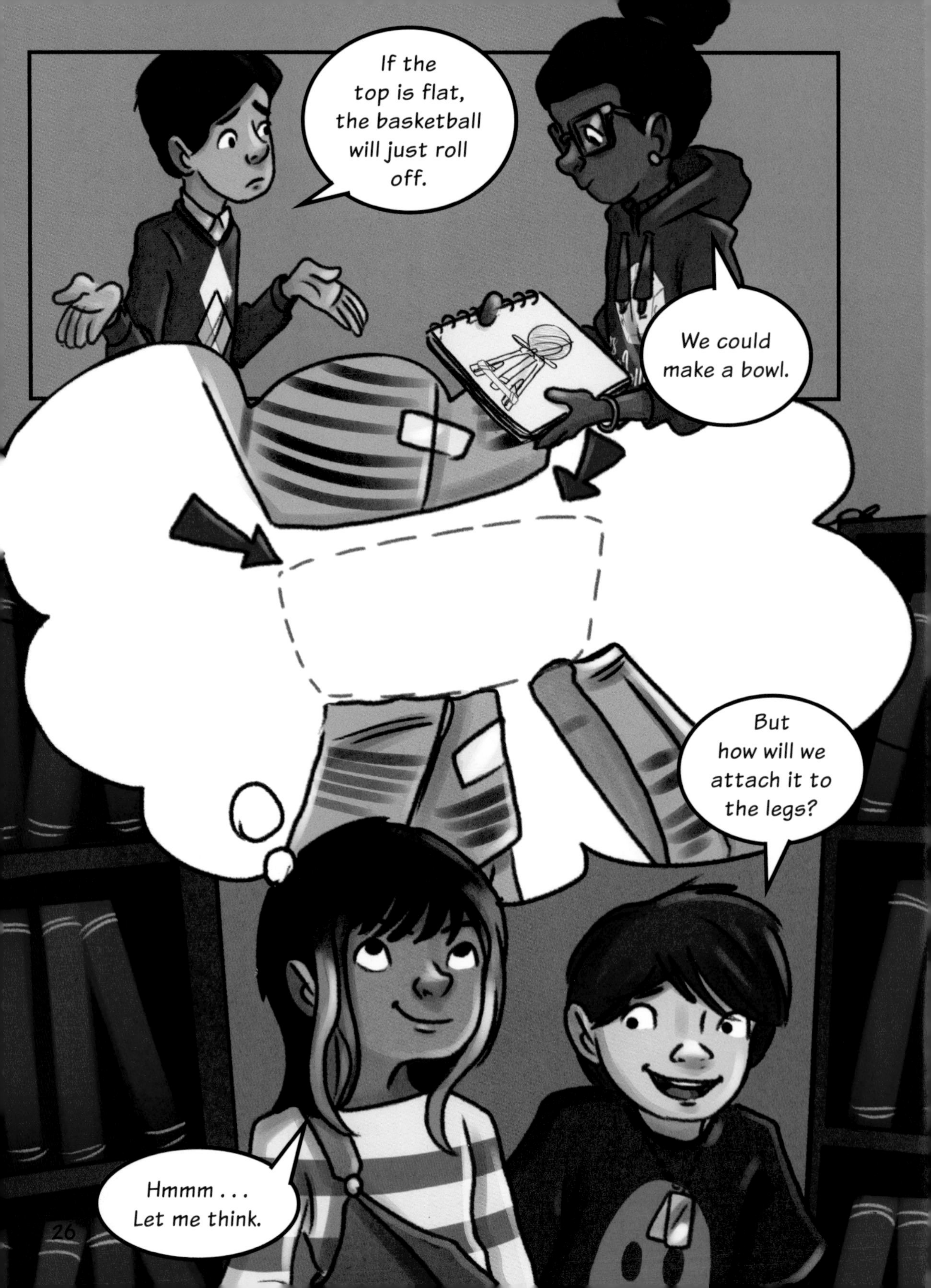
If the top is flat, the basketball will just roll off.
We could make a bowl.
But how will we attach it to the legs?
Hmmm . . . Let me think.

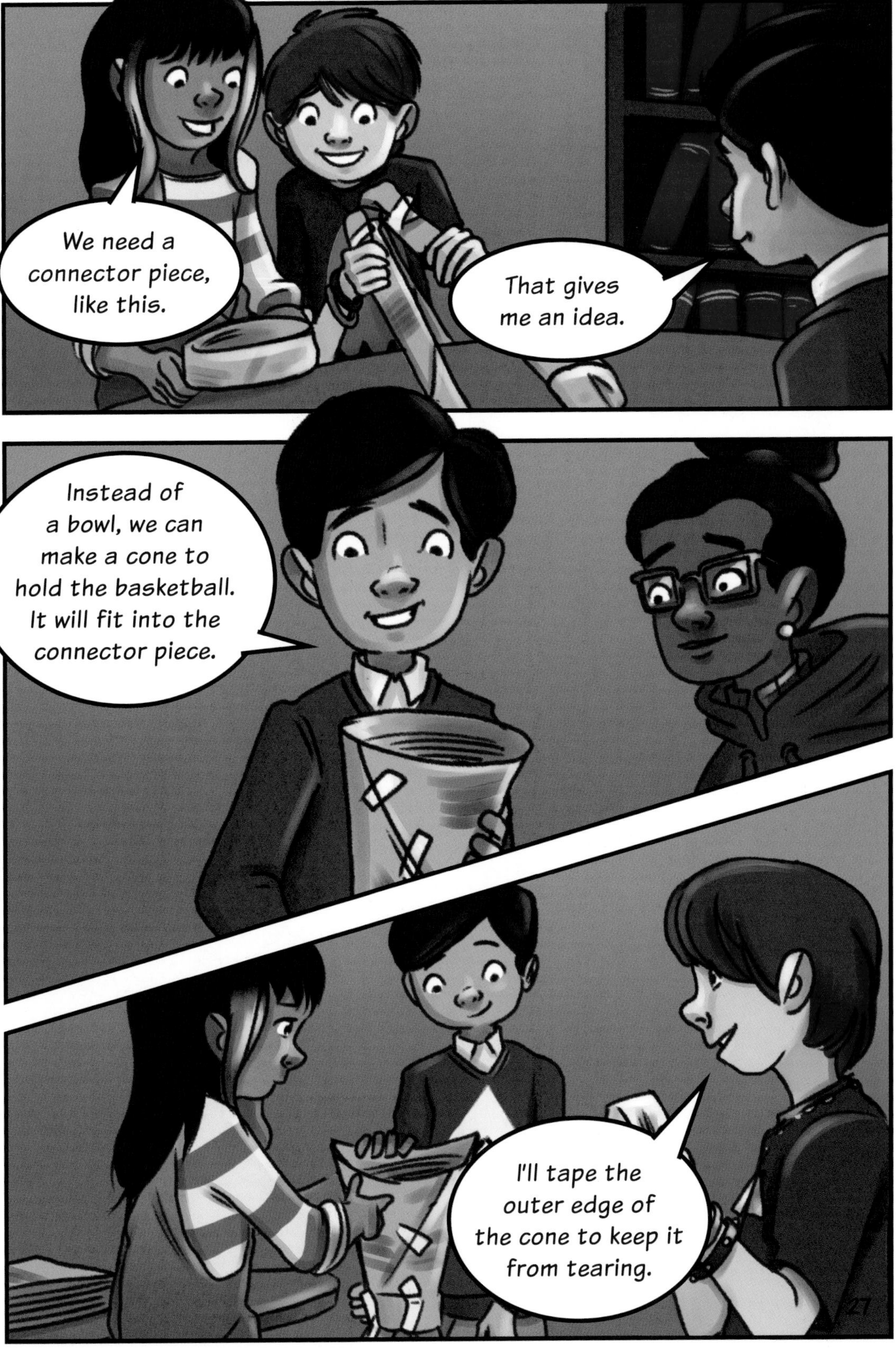
We need a connector piece, like this.
That gives me an idea.
Instead of a bowl, we can make a cone to hold the basketball. It will fit into the connector piece.
I'll tape the outer edge of the cone to keep it from tearing.

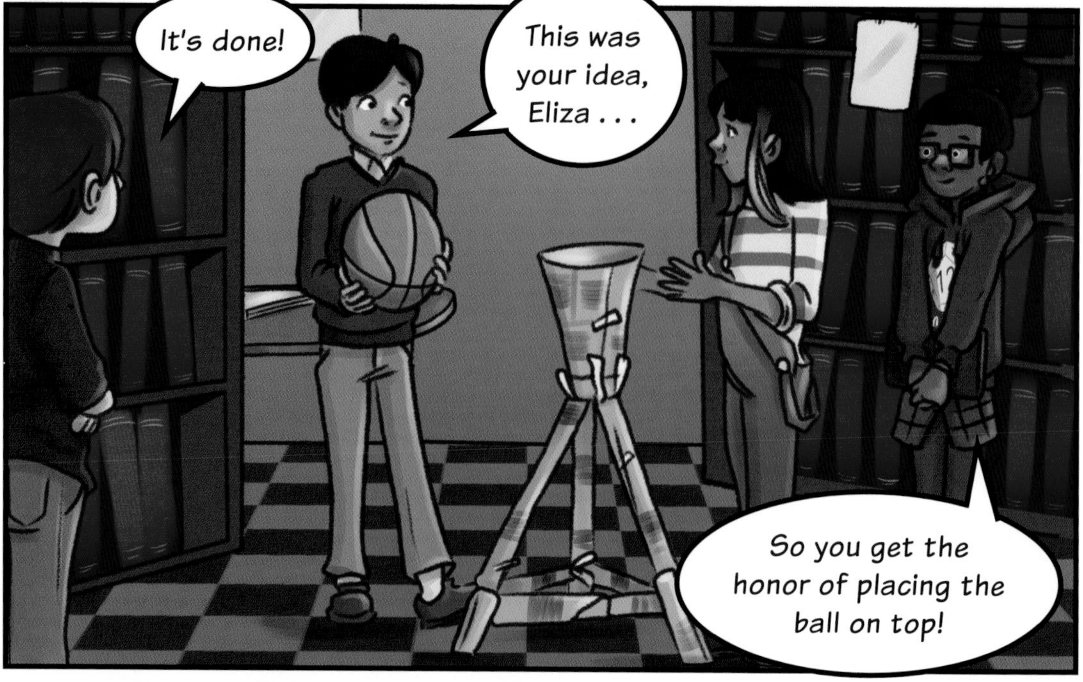
It's done!
This was your idea, Eliza . . .
So you get the honor of placing the ball on top!

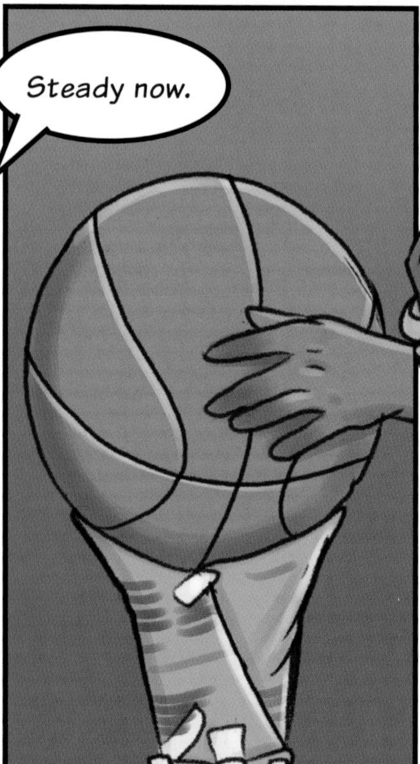
Steady now.

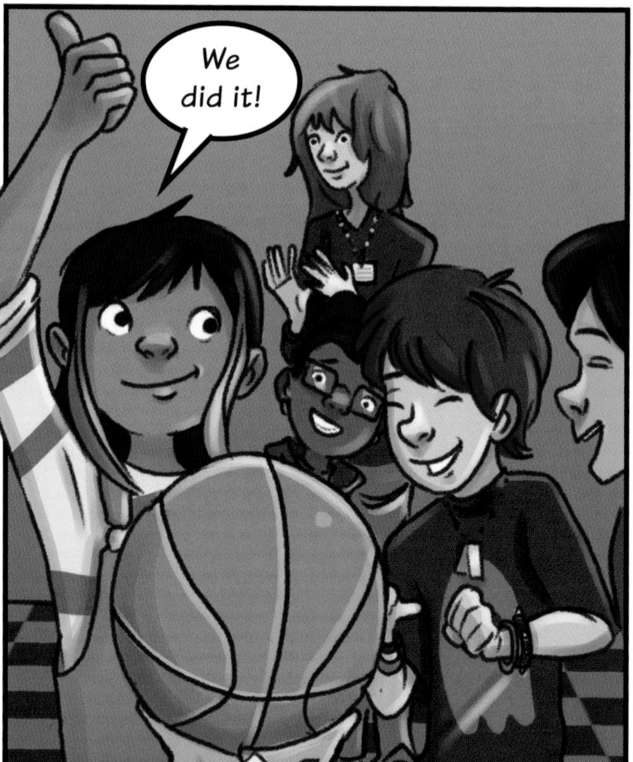
We did it!

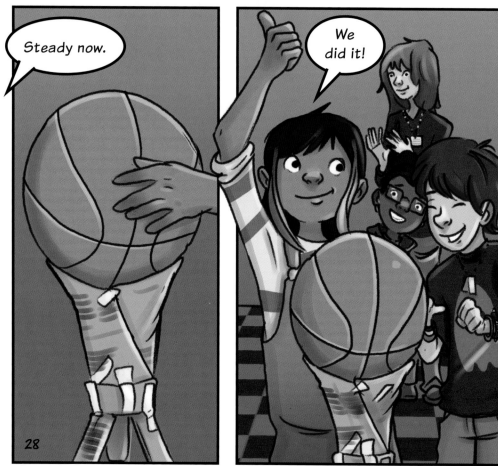

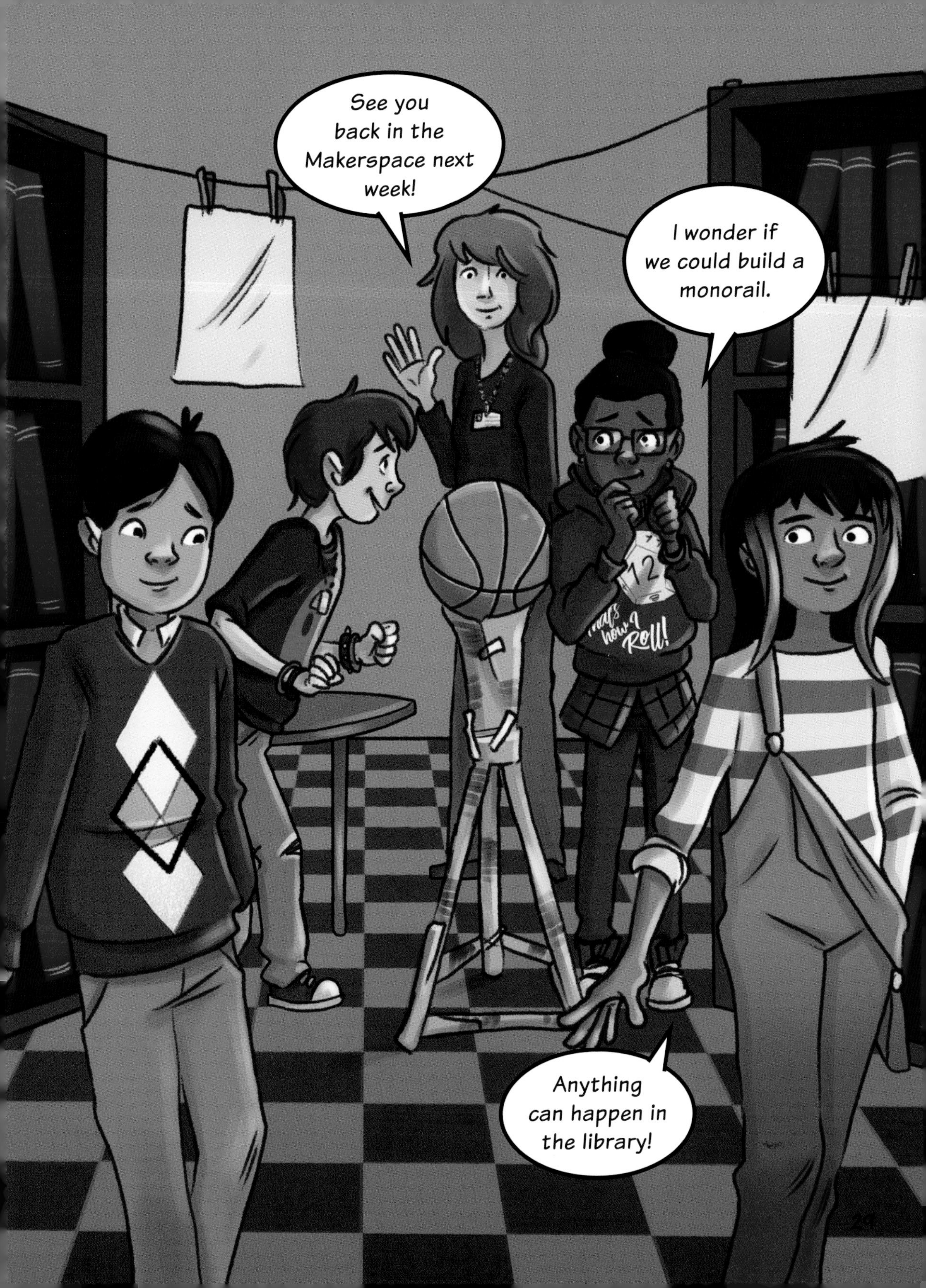
See you back in the Makerspace next week!
I wonder if we could build a monorail.
Anything can happen in the library!

GLOSSARY

catapult—device for launching objects into the air

core—center part of a building, often holding stairs or elevators

design—draw or make a plan to build something

foundation—base or support for a building

halo—circle on top of something

monorail—single rail for a train-like vehicle

CREATE YOUR OWN MAKERSPACE!

1. Find a place to store supplies. It could be a large area, like the space in this story. But it can also be a cart, bookshelf, or storage bin.

2. Make a list of supplies that you would like to have. Include items found in your recycling bin, such as cardboard boxes, tin cans, and plastic bottles (caps too!). Add art materials, household items such as rubber bands, paper clips, straws, and any other materials useful for planning, building, and creating.

3. Pass out your list to friends and parents. Ask them for help in gathering the materials.

4. It's time to create. Let your imagination run wild!

BUILD A NEWSPAPER TOWER!

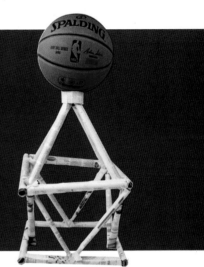

WHAT YOU NEED

- Newspaper
- Masking tape
- Balls of various sizes and weights: ping-pong ball, golf ball, tennis ball, baseball, basketball

The engineering process includes six key steps:

1. **Identify the problem:** Your problem is designing a tower that can hold up a ball.

2. **Research:** Brainstorm ideas for how to solve your problem. On page 11, Codie and Matt imagine different tower designs. Are there any other tall towers that you can think of?

3. **Plan:** From the towers you imagined, pick one with a design that will best solve your problem. Then draw a plan for how to build your tower, like Eliza did on page 23.

4. **Create:** Using the design you drew for reference, build your tower.

5. **Test:** Once your tower is built, test it out. Start with the lightest ball to see how much weight your tower can hold up. Then test out the heavier balls. If your tower wobbles or starts to collapse, move on to step six.

6. **Improve:** Brainstorm ways to fix any problems. How can you make your tower stronger or more stable? Once you make these adjustments, go back to step 5. Continue to test and improve your design to see how much weight your tower can hold!

FURTHER RESOURCES

Hurley, Michael. *The World's Most Amazing Skyscrapers.* Chicago, IL: Raintree, 2012.

Kenney, Karen Latchana. *Building a Skyscraper.* Mankato, MN: Amicus, 2019.

Miller, Shannon McClintock, and Blake Hoena. *A Low-Tech Mission.* North Mankato, MN: Capstone, 2019.

Orr, Tamra B. *The Space Needle.* Kennett Square, PA: Purple Toad, 2017.

DON'T MISS THESE EXCITING ADVENTURES IN MAKERSPACE!

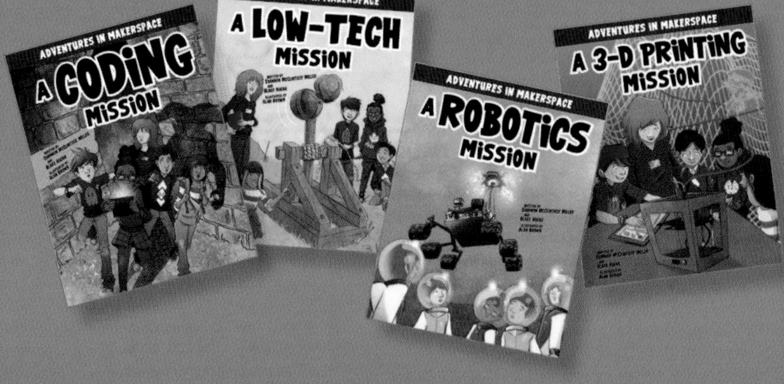

ADVENTURES IN MAKERSPACE
A CODING MISSION
ADVENTURES IN MAKERSPACE
A LOW-TECH MISSION
ADVENTURES IN MAKERSPACE
A ROBOTICS MISSION
ADVENTURES IN MAKERSPACE
A 3-D PRINTING MISSION